FABLEHAVEN

BOOK of IMAGINATION

CREATE • DISCOVER • EXPLORE

#1 NEW YORK TIMES BEST-SELLING AUTHOR

BRANDON MULL

AND _ _ _ _ _ _ _ _ _ _ _ _ _

YOUR NAME HERE

SHADOW
MOUNTAIN

To J. Tucker Davis,
a frequent nominee for the
Brandon Mull Unpaid Editorial Team
Golden Bookmark Award

Text © 2016 Creative Concepts, LC

Illustrations © 2016 Brandon Dorman, except p. 18, Chris Creek; p. 21, 34, 57, 71, 85, 117, 122–23, Steve Vistaunet; p. 30, NASA.gov; and p. 94–95, 154–55, James Fritzler. Photos of Brandon Mull, courtesy Brandon Mull. Backgrounds throughout the book from Shutterstock.

Visit us at ShadowMountain.com

ISBN 978–1–62972–241–2

Printed in the United States of America
Lake Book Manufacturing, Inc., Melrose Park, IL

10   9   8   7   6   5   4   3   2   1

Welcome.

Entering the world of Fablehaven requires an individual to think beyond the ordinary. The very fact that you have chosen to open this book means that you have an extraordinary mind.

To be sure, the pages within this volume will tap into your imagination—even stretch it. Of course, your knowledge of the world of Fablehaven and its many mythical and magical creatures, including dragons, will enhance your experience.

Remember, your imagination is endless and so are your choices. That means in a book like this your possibilities are endless.

Let your imagining begin!

—Brandon Mull

SHHH! IT'S A SECRET!

Within the pages of this book are secret codes that will help you discover a secret message from me, Brandon Mull, about Dragonwatch—the sequel series to Fablehaven. I will give you the first code here.

1:152:6:1

Notice there are four numbers to the code. The first number refers to a particular paperback volume in the Fablehaven series. The second number refers to the page in the book. The third number tells you how many lines to count from the top of the page. The final number refers to a word within that line.

For example, this first code means you're looking for volume 1, page 152, the sixth line from the top, and the first word in that line.

Follow this code and you'll have your first word. Good luck! And remember, it's a secret! Shhh.

— BRANDON MULL

Look for the remaining codes throughout this book to find the entire message. Write down the entire message on page 148.

This book belongs to

_____
sign your name like you usually do

_____
sign your name as if you are a tiny nipsie

_____
sign your name as if you just swallowed a courage potion

_____
sign your name as if you are the Fairy King or Fairy Queen

_____
sign your name as if you are a fog giant

_____
sign your name as if you are temporarily a chicken

_____
sign your name as if you are flying upside down in the talons of a griffin

_____
sign your name backwards so it can be read in a mirror

_____
sign your name in a secret fairy language

_____
sign your name as if you're being chased by a dragon

This book belongs to
the hand below.

Trace your hand on this page.

WARNING!

Do Not Read This Book Without Permission or Else . . .

_____

_____

_____

_____

_____

_____

_____

_____

Write a warning to keep away uninvited readers.

Hide This Book

A good caretaker must keep secrets. Keep this book hidden when you're not using it. Don't keep it in the same place for too long. Find the best hiding places in your house or bedroom and write them on the lines below.

_____

_____

_____

_____

_____

_____

KEEP OUT!

Write messages on these signs that will keep trespassers away from the entrance of Fablehaven.

TRESPASSERS WILL BE TURNED TO STONE

DRAW A MAP OF YOUR OWN MAGICAL PRESERVE

Where is it located? What is it called? Include your home, landmarks, trees, trails, and areas to avoid.

WHO DO YOU TRUST?

Which 6 characters from the Fablehaven series would you recruit to help you run your preserve?

1. Name: _____

2. Name: _____

3. Name: _____

4. Name: _____

5. Name: _____

6. Name: _____

WHO WILL YOU INVITE?

The Fablehaven register is a magical book that controls access in and out of the preserve. When a visitor's name is written in the register, the spells protecting Fablehaven from intruders are lifted for that individual.

Now it's your turn. Create a register for your magical preserve. Write the names of friends and family you would like to invite into your preserve.

CREATE A "HELP WANTED" AD FOR YOUR NEW MAGICAL PRESERVE.

Classified Ads

_____ Preserve is looking for a new _____. Long hours. Good pay. Must _____, have previous experience with _____, _____, and _____. Other prerequisites include the ability to think fast, work hard, and _____. Familiarity with _____ languages a plus. Following rules is a must. On the job training is available for the following three skills: _____, _____, and _____. Bonus pay is available for surviving the first two weeks. Paid time off for Midsummer's Eve. Additional talents or achievements that will give you an edge over other applicants include _____

_____

_____

_____

_____

_____

Create a Codename

SOMETIMES CARETAKERS MUST GO UNDERCOVER. CREATE A CODENAME FOR YOURSELF AND FIVE FRIENDS.

YOUR CODE NAME

_____

FRIEND #1

_____

FRIEND #2

_____

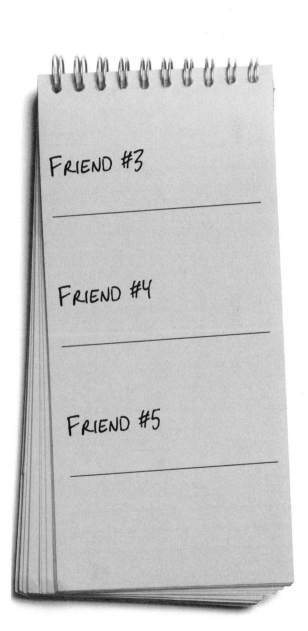

FRIEND #3

_____

FRIEND #4

_____

FRIEND #5

_____

3:303:6:1

Some magical preserves have their own currency.
Design a gold coin to use on your preserve.

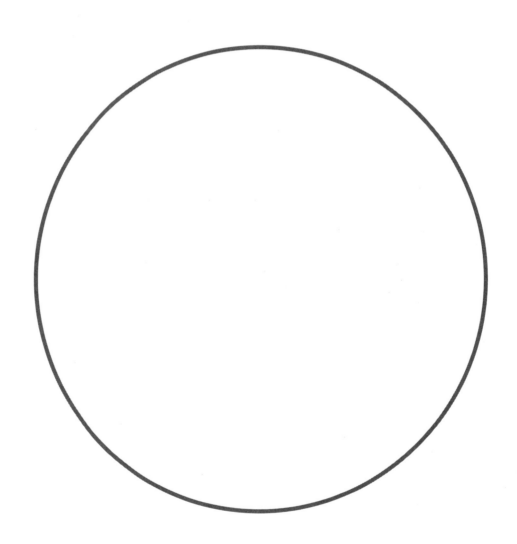

THE IMAGINATION IS A MUSCLE. IF IT IS NOT EXERCISED, IT ATROPHIES.

—NEIL GAIMAN

KNOW YOUR KNOTS

Muriel the witch was imprisoned in an ivy shack with magical knots. A good caretaker should know the basics of knot tying. Find a rope and tie the knot below.

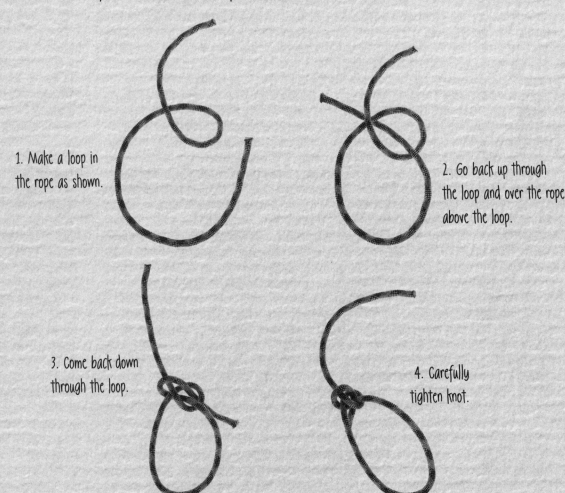

1. Make a loop in the rope as shown.

2. Go back up through the loop and over the rope above the loop.

3. Come back down through the loop.

4. Carefully tighten knot.

Grandpa Sorenson loves to use this bowline knot. This knot makes a reasonably secure loop in the end of a piece of rope and is useful as part of a snare to catch a mischievous imp or as part of a makeshift bow and arrow. Note: Two bowlines can be linked together to join two ropes.

ASK THE
TOTEM WALL

You have found the legendary Totem Wall. Do you need an answer to an important question? The magical Totem Wall can help. What question will you ask? Write your question below.

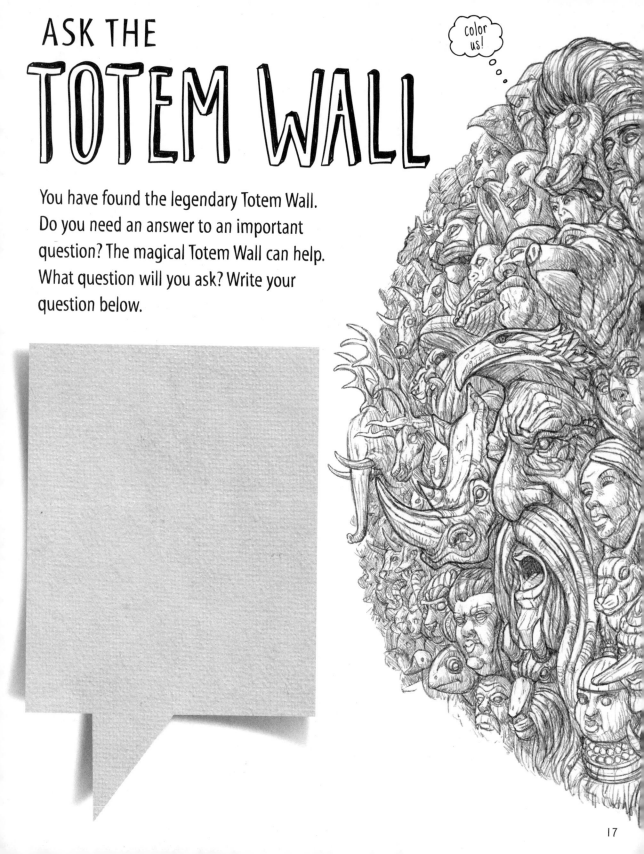

color us!

DRAW A DRAGON'S HEAD

Follow the step-by-step illustrations below.

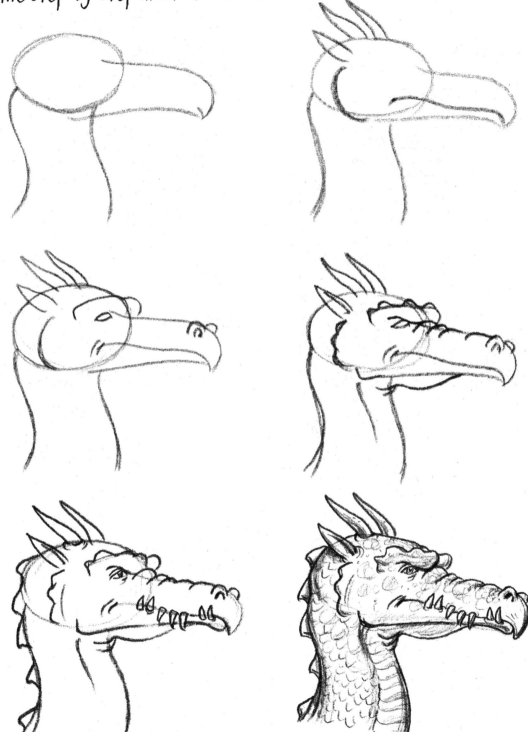

Now it's your turn. Create your own dragon head.

Dragons can create paralyzing fear. Imagine that your hands and arms are paralyzed from encountering a dragon, but you still need to write a message. Use your feet or mouth to write a note on this page.

Color this dryad—guardian of the Fairy Shrine.

BECOME A POTION MASTER LIKE TANU

If you could drink a courage potion, what would you want to do?

If you could give someone a love potion, who would you give it to?

If you could double your height with an enlarger potion, what would you do?

If you could take a shrinking potion, where would you hide?

4:404:3:8

MAKE A POTION

Circle five items to create your own potion.

What will it do to the person who drinks it? _____

What will you call it? _____

Spicy Mustard	Oregano	Worcestershire Sauce
Grape Soda	Beef Broth	Ghost Chili Pepper
Chili Powder	Powdered Sugar	Blueberry Yogurt
Cornflakes	Chocolate Syrup	Barbecue Sauce
Ground Pepper	Pickle Juice	Corn Syrup
Skim Milk	Ketchup	Oatmeal
Tomato Juice	Vanilla	Lemon Juice
Molasses	Honey	Lime Juice
Salad Dressing	Tabasco Sauce	Melted Popsicle
Raisins	Cinnamon	Gummy Bears

REACH THE HIDDEN POND

Travel from the Caretaker's house in Fablehaven to the Hidden Pond, home to the Shrine of the Fairy Queen. Beware of creatures that will try to stop you. Cut out the die on page 156, then fold and tape it together.

The last person who drank some milk rolls first. Each person takes a turn rolling the die. Follow the directions on the die. Use a piece of cereal or candy as your token to journey to the Hidden Pond. The first person to reach the Hidden Pond wins!

Note: If you are mortal, you are not permitted to step upon this hallowed ground—unless you are Fairykind, of course!

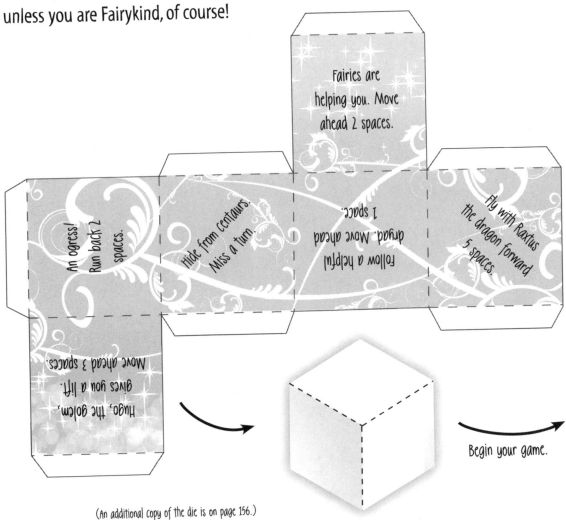

Begin your game.

(An additional copy of the die is on page 156.)

Hidden Pond

Caretaker's house

Bake a Dessert

Practice being a brownie and make something imaginative using the following ingredients:

1½ tablespoons milk

1 stick butter

3 large eggs

1¼ cups flour

1 cup sugar

¼ teaspoon baking soda

1 teaspoon vanilla

1 cup chopped pecans

20 caramels

3 cups milk chocolate chips

Now decide what it will look like!

Cookies? Bake at 375° F. for 8 min.

Cupcakes? Bake at 375° F. for 15 min.

Brownies? Bake at 350° F. for 30 min. or until a toothpick inserted in the center comes out clean.

DRAW AN IMP

Seth learned the hard way to never leave a fairy indoors overnight. In the empty jars below, draw what each fairy would look like as an imp.

Write as many words as you can that use the letters from the word **FABLEHAVEN**. Words must be three or more letters. We found sixty. How many can you find?

FABLEHAVEN

have
fab
van

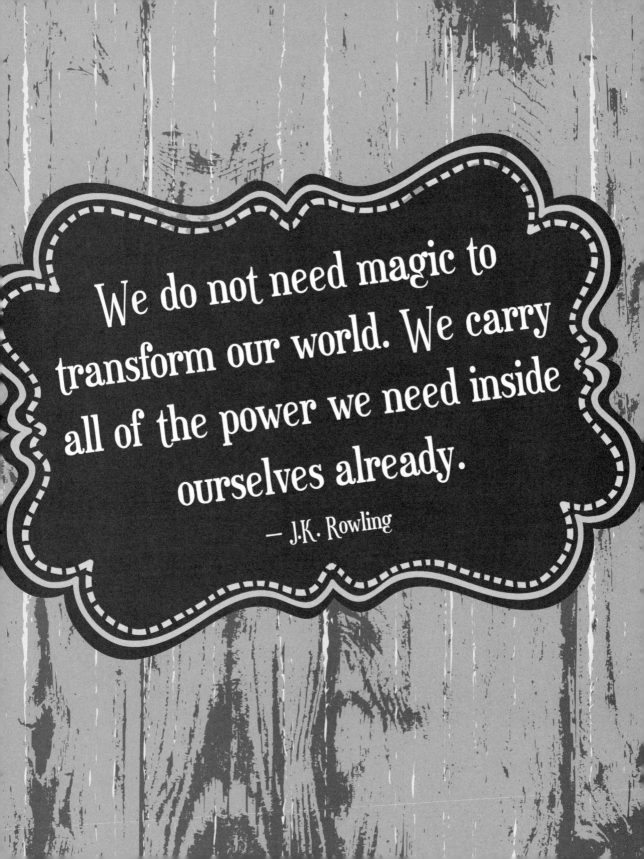

We do not need magic to transform our world. We carry all of the power we need inside ourselves already.

— J.K. Rowling

MAKE A RAIN STICK

KENDRA ACQUIRES A REAL RAIN STICK AT THE
LOST MESA PRESERVE. MAKE YOUR OWN RAIN STICK.

2. TRACE THE END OF YOUR TUBE ONTO A PIECE OF CONSTRUCTION PAPER.
DRAW A SECOND CIRCLE THAT IS TWO TIMES BIGGER THAN YOUR FIRST CIRCLE AND
THEN DRAW FOUR SPOKES BETWEEN THE TWO CIRCLES. CUT OUT THE OUTER
CIRCLE. CUT ALONG THE SPOKES.

1. GET A LONG CARDBOARD
TUBE (MAILING, PAPER TOWEL,
OR WRAPPING PAPER TUBE).

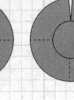

3. COVER ONE END OF YOUR TUBE WITH THE
CONSTRUCTION PAPER AND TAPE SHUT.

5. CRUNCH THE
ALUMINUM FOIL
PIECES INTO LONG,
THIN, SNAKE-LIKE
SHAPES. THEN
TWIST EACH ONE
INTO A SPRING
SHAPE.

6. PUT THE ALUMINUM FOIL SPRINGS INTO YOUR TUBE.

4. CUT A FEW
PIECES OF ALUMINUM
FOIL THAT ARE
ABOUT ONE AND A
HALF TIMES THE
LENGTH OF YOUR
TUBE AND ABOUT SIX
INCHES WIDE.

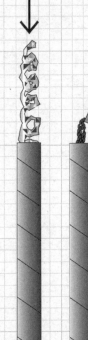

7. POUR A HANDFUL OF DRY BEANS, DRY RICE,
OR UNPOPPED POPCORN KERNELS INTO YOUR
TUBE. EXPERIMENT TO SEE HOW DIFFERENT
AMOUNTS AND DIFFERENT TYPES OF SEEDS AND
BEANS CHANGE THE SOUND.

8. MAKE ANOTHER CAP FROM CONSTRUC-
TION PAPER AND SEAL THE TOP OF YOUR
TUBE. DECORATE THE TUBE WITH COLORED
CONSTRUCTION PAPER, MARKERS,
PAINT, OR CRAYONS.

9. WRAP YARN AROUND ONE END OF THE RAIN STICK
AND LET THE ENDS HANG DOWN. ADD FEATHERS,
BEADS, OR OTHER DECORATIONS AS DESIRED.

CARVE A PUMPKIN

Guard against the vile creatures that appear on Midsummer's Eve by designing your own fairy lanterns. What will the faces of your jack-o'-lanterns look like? Draw four faces below.

NAVIGATE THE MAZE

The centaurs of Fablehaven live at Grunhold. Their unicorn horn is protected by an invisible Tauran Maze. Find your way through the maze and retrieve the horn.

Use a wax candle like a piece of chalk
to write a secret message.

Color the fairies. You don't see them? Better drink the milk.

Write the words.

Just like Seth, you were caught trading batteries with Newel and Doren. Write the following sentence "I will not trade batteries with the satyrs" until the page is full. (Hint: Does that mean writing the sentence 30 times or 1 time? You decide.)

TOP RECRUITS

FOR MEMBERS OF THE KNIGHTS OF THE DAWN

Find pictures of people in magazines, catalogs, or newspapers. Cut them out and attach them to this page.

Brandon

Brandon getting inspiration for a griffin from the natural world.

Falcon

2:203:3:1

Ogre Stew

The ogress of Fablehaven loves to cook. Her specialty is Ogre Stew. Now it's your turn. Follow the recipe below. This may require adult supervision. When your stew is finished, copy the sign on the next page and invite your friends or family to taste the stew.

Ingredients
  1 pound beef round roast, cut into 1-inch pieces
  2 tablespoons all-purpose flour
  2 tablespoons vegetable oil
  2 medium onions, chopped
  2 cloves garlic, finely chopped
  1 can beef stock
  2 cups water
  2 teaspoons Worcestershire sauce
  4 cups baby red potatoes, halved
  3 carrots, sliced

Directions
Toss beef with flour; set aside.

Heat oil in a large pot over medium heat and brown beef. Remove beef from pot; set aside.

Stir onions and garlic into same pot and cook, stirring frequently, until onions are tender, about 4 minutes. Stir in beef stock, water, Worcestershire sauce, and beef. Bring to a boil over high heat. Reduce heat to low and simmer, covered, stirring occasionally, 40 minutes or until beef is almost tender. Stir in potatoes and carrots and simmer an additional 40 minutes or until beef and vegetables are tender.

Now serving Ogre Stew.

Price: _____ per bowl.

All proceeds go to

_____.

I WILL NEVER WAKE A SLEEPING DRAGON WITH A HOT FIRE POKER.

After Seth discovers that the fablehaven woods are full of potentially deadly mythical and magical creatures, he promises to never go into the woods again. Think of something potentially deadly and commit today that you will never do that thing. For example, *I will never smoke cigarettes. I will never play hopscotch on the freeway. I will never wake a sleeping dragon with a hot fire poker.* Write your "I will never" statement here.

_____

_____

_____

_____

_____

_____

_____

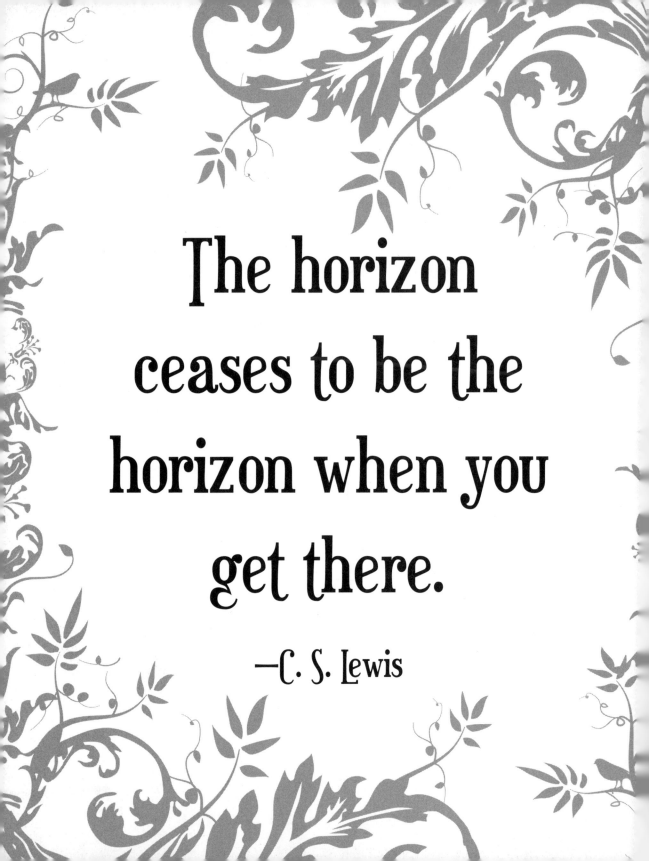

The horizon ceases to be the horizon when you get there.

—C. S. Lewis

Try to turn
this page with
your mind.

Congratulations! You succeeded!

You used your mind to guide your hand.

A stingbulb of my own!

This magical fruit has the ability to clone a person. If you had a stingbulb clone of yourself for three days, what would your clone do?

HIDDEN MESSAGE

There is a hidden message at the very end of the first book in the Fablehaven series. What does it say? Write the message on the sheet below.

(Hint: It is written near the bottom edge on the last page of the final chapter of volume one.)

THE GUARDIAN

your family pet is now the guardian of a hidden, ancient magical artifact. Draw your pet in its new role as a guardian. What special power does your pet have to protect the treasure it is guarding?

There is great power in harboring a single goal.

—The Sphinx

Keys to the Demon Prison by Brandon Mull

TRAP THE MAGIC

Fairies like to look at their reflections. Leprechauns love treasure. Using items around your house, build a fairy trap or a leprechaun trap. Take a picture of it and attach it here—or draw the design here. Be creative.

MAGICAL WEB

The fairies of Fablehaven threaded magical rope back and forth to create a magical web, trapping the demon Bahumat under the Forgotten Chapel. Follow the instructions to weave your own magical web.

Materials needed
- yarn
- clear tape

Choose a colorful yarn to use to build the web. Then choose a spot for the web — indoors or outdoors.

Make the arms of the web
First, make a large X out of yarn. Secure the ends to the walls, cabinet, swing set, tree, or other items where you're building your web. Make additional crisscrossing lines, matching up the middles and securing each end as you go.

Make the web rings
Cut a very long strand of yarn. Tie the end near the center of your web, then stretch the yarn around to each arm and simply loop it around. You don't need to tie knots—keep it fast and easy. Don't try to be accurate and precise. It's okay if the web looks unfinished in places. When you run out of yarn, tie the end with a knot, and start with another strand. Continue this process to create as many rings as you like.

What would you do with your very own magical artifact?

If you had ONE chance to use the Sands of Sanctity—which can heal anyone from anything—who would you heal and why?

_____

_____

_____

If you had ONE chance to use the Chronometer— which can transport you through time—would you travel to the past or the future? What year? Why?

_____

_____

_____

If you had ONE chance to use the Oculus—which allows you to see anywhere—what would you choose to look at? Why?

_____

_____

_____

If you had ONE chance to use the Translocator—which gives you the ability to transport yourself and three individuals to any place you have visited previously—where would you go? Who would you take with you?

_____

_____

_____

If you had the chance to use the Font of Immortality—which grants immortality to the person who drinks from it at least once a week—would you choose to use it? Why? (Remember, your family and friends would get older and eventually die, but you wouldn't.)

_____

_____

_____

A GRIFFIN, A LEPRECHAUN, AND A SACK OF GOLD.
TEST YOUR SKILLS AS A CARETAKER.

Do you have the intellect to be a caretaker of Fablehaven? Solve this caretaker problem. You have a griffin, a leprechaun, and a sack of gold. You must transport all three of them to the other side of Fablehaven—but you can only take one of them at a time. If you leave the griffin with the leprechaun, it will eat him. If you leave the leprechaun with the gold, he will steal it. How can you get all three to the other side of Fablehaven safely? Write your answer below.

_____

_____

_____

_____

(Stumped? See answer on page 148.)

Write as many words as you can that use the letters from the word DRAGONWATCH. Words must be three or more letters. We found 120 words. How many can you find?

DRAGONWATCH

drag
watch
ton

Who's a Magical Creature?

Have you ever met someone who might be a magical creature in disguise?

Who? _____

What might they be? _____

Have you ever seen an animal that might be a magical creature in disguise?

What kind of animal? _____

What might it actually be? _____

Astrids communicate telepathically. This one says, Color me.

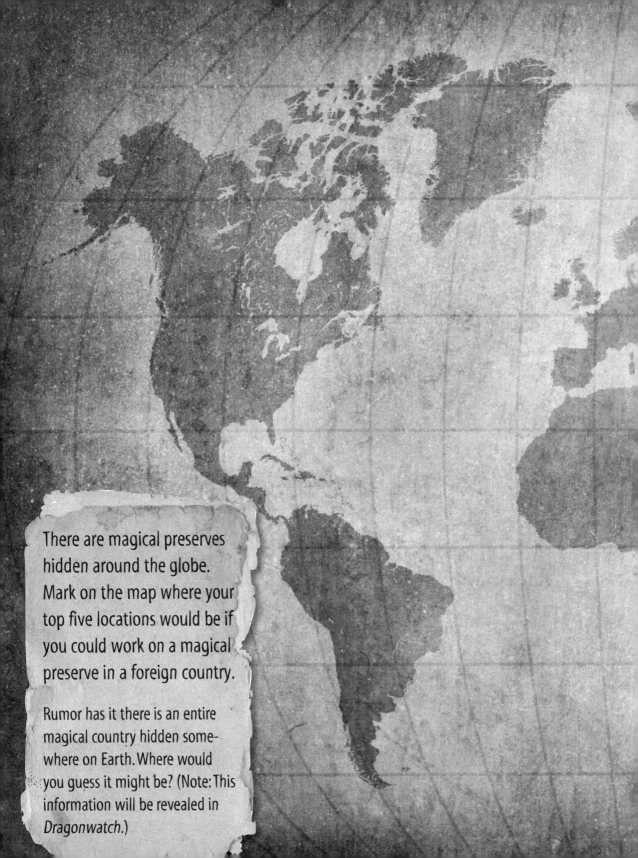

There are magical preserves hidden around the globe. Mark on the map where your top five locations would be if you could work on a magical preserve in a foreign country.

Rumor has it there is an entire magical country hidden somewhere on Earth. Where would you guess it might be? (Note: This information will be revealed in *Dragonwatch*.)

Brandon

Camouflage shirt

Survival kit

Brandon's little brother Bryson, with his camo shirt and survival kit, helped inspire some of the descriptions of Seth.

Make a Unicorn Horn

STEP 1: CUT OUT PATTERN.

STEP 2: ROLL LENGTHWISE AND TAPE.

STEP 3: DECORATE WITH STICKY GEMS OR GLITTER.

STEP 4: PUNCH A TINY HOLE ON EITHER SIDE OF THE BOTTOM OF THE HORN, THREAD AN ELASTIC CORD THROUGH, AND SECURE WITH KNOTS.

TOP RECRUITS

FOR MEMBERS OF THE
SOCIETY OF THE EVENING STAR

Find pictures of people in magazines, catalogs, or newspapers. Cut them out and attach them to this page.

LEARN TO MAKE WISE CHOICES

Lesson #1

MAKING MISTAKES IS PART OF LEARNING TO CHOOSE WELL.

—Patton Burgess
World's Greatest Adventurer

If you'd like, cut out the quote from
Patton Burgess on the previous page
and post it where you will see it often.

Midsummer's Eve is a time of celebration and wild abandon for the creatures of Fablehaven. Draw a creature that you think would appear on Midsummer's Eve.

Draw a Magic Circle

Grandpa Sorenson protects his grandchildren by putting magic salt around their beds. Draw a circle of magic salt around this bed. Make sure your circle is complete. Imagine yourself inside the circle. Close your eyes. Take a deep breath. Feel the peace of knowing that nothing bad is able to cross the circle. Draw, write, or create chaos outside the circle, but remember that you are inside the circle. You are impervious to evil. You are safe. Good night, and sweet dreams.

MY BABY HYDRA

Hydras are often found in lakes. Draw a home for your hydra, then use a pencil to poke holes in the outlines of the five circles. Insert your fingers into the holes to create a five-headed hydra.

This fairy is staring in a mirror. Color her beautifully.

I AM AWESOME!

In case anyone ever doubted your ability to be an awesome caretaker of a magical preserve, finish this letter with adjectives and verbs that describe you best.

To whom it may concern,

I am qualified to be the caretaker of this magical preserve because people tell me all the time that I am _____ . I can _____
(personality adjective)   (verb)
fast, and I am very _____ when it comes to danger. I am
                    (personality adjective)
reliable, trustworthy, and _____ . In addition, I know that
                           (personality adjective)
it's important to _____ and always obey the rules. For the record,
                  (verb)
my nickname is _____ . If that doesn't
               (adjective + animal #1 + adjective + animal #2)
make the creatures of Fablehaven _____ , I don't know what will.
                                 (verb)
One time I came face-to-face with a _____ dragon who
                                    (appearance adjective)
_____ me, but thanks to my _____ face and my
(verb, past tense)   (appearance adjective)
_____ muscles, I was able to escape and _____ . Yes, I
(appearance adjective)   (verb)
am definitely a _____ caretaker!
                (adjective)

I AM AWESOME!

This time, ask <u>someone else</u> to supply the adjectives and verbs. Write them in the spaces provided.

To whom it may concern,

I am qualified to be the caretaker of this magical preserve because people tell me all the time that I am ＿＿＿＿＿＿＿＿. I can ＿＿＿＿＿＿
(personality adjective)   (verb)
fast, and I am very ＿＿＿＿＿＿＿＿ when it comes to danger. I am
(personality adjective)
reliable, trustworthy, and ＿＿＿＿＿＿＿＿. In addition, I know that
(personality adjective)
it's important to ＿＿＿＿＿ and always obey the rules. For the record,
(verb)
my nickname is ＿＿＿＿＿＿＿＿＿＿＿＿＿＿＿＿. If that doesn't
(adjective + animal #1 + adjective + animal #2)
make the creatures of Fablehaven ＿＿＿＿＿, I don't know what will.
(verb)
One time I came face-to-face with a ＿＿＿＿＿＿＿＿ dragon who
(appearance adjective)
＿＿＿＿＿＿＿ me, but thanks to my ＿＿＿＿＿＿＿＿ face and my
(verb, past tense)   (appearance adjective)
＿＿＿＿＿＿＿＿ muscles, I was able to escape and ＿＿＿＿＿. Yes, I
(appearance adjective)   (verb)
am definitely a ＿＿＿＿＿＿＿ caretaker!
(adjective)

Beat Bubda in a Game of Dice.

Bubda

Ones	☐	3 Of a Kind	☐
Twos	☐	4 Of a Kind	☐
Threes	☐	2 Of a Kind & 3 Of a Kind	☐
Fours	☐	4 Numbers in a Sequence	☐
Fives	☐	5 Numbers in a Sequence	☐
Sixes	☐	5 Of a Kind	☐
		Total	☐

Step 1: Roll 5 dice for Bubda. Add up the numbers that match one of the categories. You may roll the dice up to three times per turn. Step 2: Roll for yourself.

_____
(your name here)

Ones ☐	**3 Of a Kind** ☐
Twos ☐	**4 Of a Kind** ☐
Threes ☐	**2 Of a Kind & 3 Of a Kind** ☐
Fours ☐	**4 Numbers in a Sequence** ☐
Fives ☐	**5 Numbers in a Sequence** ☐
Sixes ☐	**5 Of a Kind** ☐
	Total ☐

Black Cat GUARDIAN

In book one of Fablehaven, one of the five hidden ancient artifacts is protected by the Black Cat Guardian. Draw the nine lives or incarnations of the Guardian.

The first life: a life-sized, glass-black cat

The second life: a super-sized, menacing feline

The third life: a lynx with long sharp claws, tufted ears, and intimidating teeth

The fourth life: a larger and more aggressive version of the lynx

The fifth life: a panther

The sixth life: a larger and more ferocious panther

The seventh life: a panther as tall as a horse with dagger-like claws and saber-toothed fangs; four writhing, venomous black serpents sprout from its shoulders

The eighth life: like the seventh life, but without serpents and with two heads that spit black sludge that burns like acid

The ninth life: a terrifying, gargantuan cat with twelve serpents along its back; three heads, three tails, wings, and also spits acid

If the guardian had one more life, what would the incarnation look like?

If you owned an invisibility glove, how would you use it? (Remember, you'd only be invisible when standing perfectly still).

Riddles from the Sphinx

In order to pass by the Sphinx safely, you'll need to answer its riddles. Test your mind with these riddles.

1. I am the beginning of the end and the end of the universe. I am essential to Fablehaven, and I surround every preserve. What am I?

2. I have streets but no stoplights. I have cities but no buildings. I have forests but no trees. I have lakes but no water. What am I?

3. What kind of room has no doors or windows?

4. There were ten naiads in the Hidden Pond. Patton lured one out, four drowned, and five swam away. How many naiads were left?

(Confused? See answers on page 148.)

And above all, watch with glittering eyes the whole world around you because the greatest secrets are always hidden in the most unlikely places. Those who don't believe in magic will never find it.

—Roald Dahl

In ancient times, Dragonwatch was a group of wizards, enchantresses, dragon slayers, and others who confined the majority of dragons to sanctuaries. They had a special crest to identify the group. Draw a special crest or coat of arms for your own preserve.

SOLVE THIS
FABLEHAVEN ANAGRAM

RESISTS SIGNING

Flip the words and write your answer below.

_____   _____

Note: You will run into this again in Dragonwatch,
the sequel series to Fablehaven.

(Need help? Answer is on page 148.)

Cut out this mask for the next time you attend a meeting as a member of the Knights of the Dawn.

5:76:4:2

Color this replica of art found inside the Dragon Sanctuary at Wyrmroost.

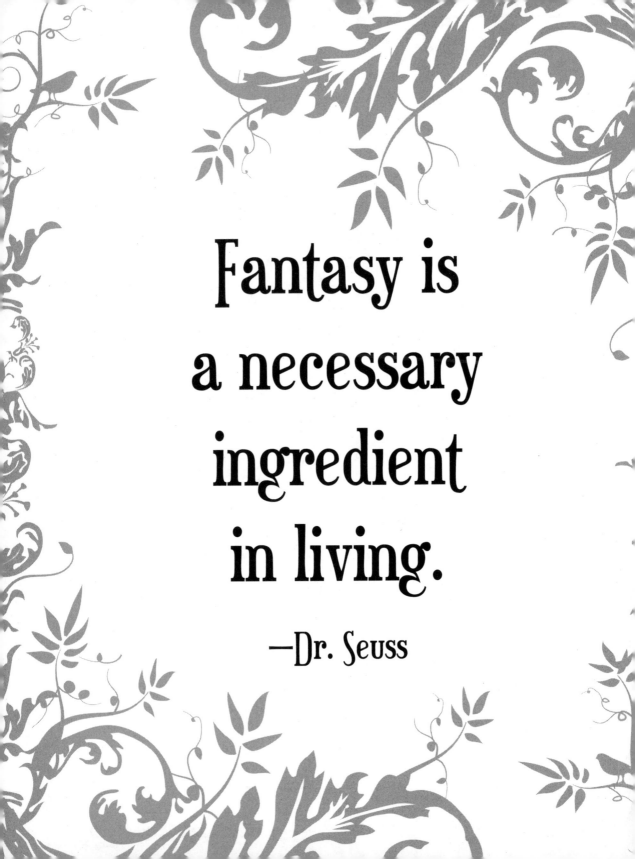

Fantasy is a necessary ingredient in living.

—Dr. Seuss

Can you withstand a distracter spell?

This exercise is meant to help strengthen your mind against distracter spells. Concentrate on the square above. Now close your eyes. Raise your hand above your head and, with your pointer finger, try to touch the center of the square. Did you succeed? Try it again, but this time close your eyes and spin around three times. How well did you do? The wizard Agad placed a much stronger distracter spell on page 141. Good luck!

Have a staring contest with this page.

Ready. Set. Go. Record your times below.

_____ _____ _____

_____ _____ _____

_____ _____ _____

_____ _____ _____

2:219:17:8

Patience mimics the power of infinity. And nobody can win a staring contest with infinity. No matter how long you last, infinity is just getting started.

—The Sphinx
Rise of the Evening Star by Brandon Mull

Create your own Raxtus

cut dark solid lines

mountain fold dotted lines

valley fold dashed lines

(A copy of this pattern that you can cut out is on pages 153–54.)

Follow the directions on the next page.

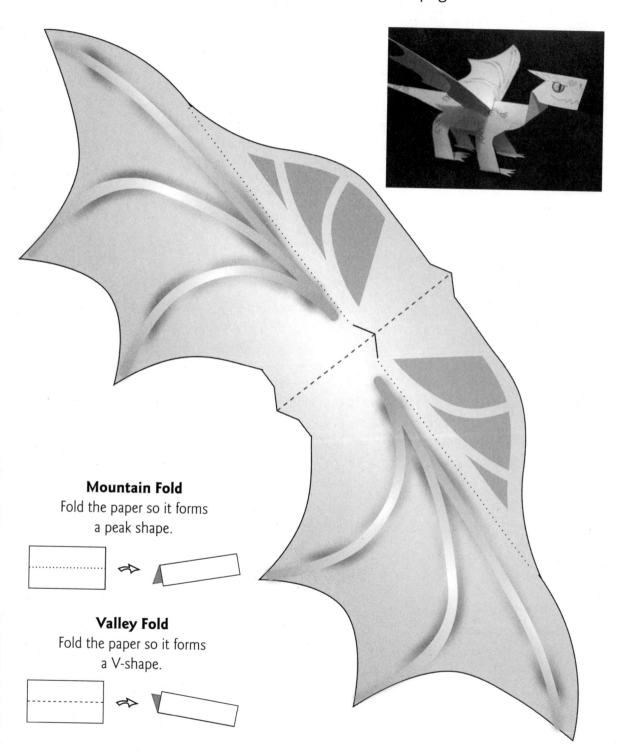

Mountain Fold
Fold the paper so it forms
a peak shape.

Valley Fold
Fold the paper so it forms
a V-shape.

Paper Raxtus Folding Directions

Body Assembly

1. Cut along the solid lines around the outside edges of the dragon.

2. For the back and head:
   - Fold the model in half along the dotted line that runs from the head to the tail.
   - Cut along the two solid lines in the middle of the back (this creates the wing slot).
   - Cut along the solid line on the top of the head (this creates a triangular horn).

3. For the legs:
   - Cut along the solid lines on the sides of the legs, including the solid line that creates a tab for the underbelly.
   - Fold on the dotted line running between the legs.

4. For the wing slot on the back:
   - Create a V-shaped space by folding a mountain fold along the dotted lines on both sides.
   - Fold a valley fold in the opposite direction along the dashed line in the middle.

5. For the neck:
   - Flatten the model.
   - Fold the head along the dotted lines (mountain fold) on both sides.
   - Fold the neck in the opposite direction (valley fold) along the dashed lines on both sides.
   - Refold the model along the dotted line between the point of the head and the tail, being sure to maintain the V-shaped space made in step 4.

6. Fold the feet inward along the dotted lines so they go under the dragon.

7. Slide together the two tabs to create the underbelly and connect the two sides of the model.

Wing Assembly

1. Cut around the solid lines on the outside of the wings.
2. Fold lengthwise along the dotted line (mountain fold).
3. Fold crosswise along the dashed line (valley fold).
4. With the wings still folded in half, cut along the solid line.
5. Insert the wings into the V-shaped space in the back of the dragon body and unfold slightly to fill the space.

If dragons weren't freaky, they'd be disappointing.

–Seth

Secrets of the Dragon Sanctuary by Brandon Mull

SOLVE THE MAZE

The Knights of the Dawn must enter the Dreamstone and solve the maze in order to find a hidden key.

LEARN TO MAKE WISE CHOICES

Lesson #2

DO NOT OBSESS OVER CHOICES YOU CANNOT CHANGE. MISTAKES HAPPEN. LEARN FROM THE PAST, BUT CONCENTRATE ON THE PRESENT AND FUTURE.

—Patton Burgess
World's Greatest Adventurer

*If you'd like, cut out the quote from
Patton Burgess on the previous page
and post it where you will see it often.*

Make Wizard Slime

Wizard slime comes in a variety of colors. The most potent is orange. Created by wizards, this slimy substance is effective in drawing out poison from infected tissue. But even without a wizard's spell, mortals will have fun playing with this slimy goo.

SUPPLIES:

2 (4-ounce) bottles of
   Elmer's Glue
1 teaspoon Borax (found in the
   laundry detergent section of
   the grocery store)

Water
Plastic Cup
Bowl
Food Coloring

DIRECTIONS:

1. Gather all supplies.

2. Empty the two bottles of glue into a bowl. Fill bottles with warm water and shake. Empty into the bowl.

3. Add desired food coloring. Set bowl aside.

4. In your cup combine 1/2 cup warm water and Borax and mix until Borax dissolves. Then pour mixture into your glue bowl.

5. Start stirring. Mixture will become stringy. Keep mixing by using your hands and squishing around. After a few minutes, it should be pretty gelatinous.

6. Play with it for a bit, and it will become the perfect GOOEY consistency! So fun and so easy!

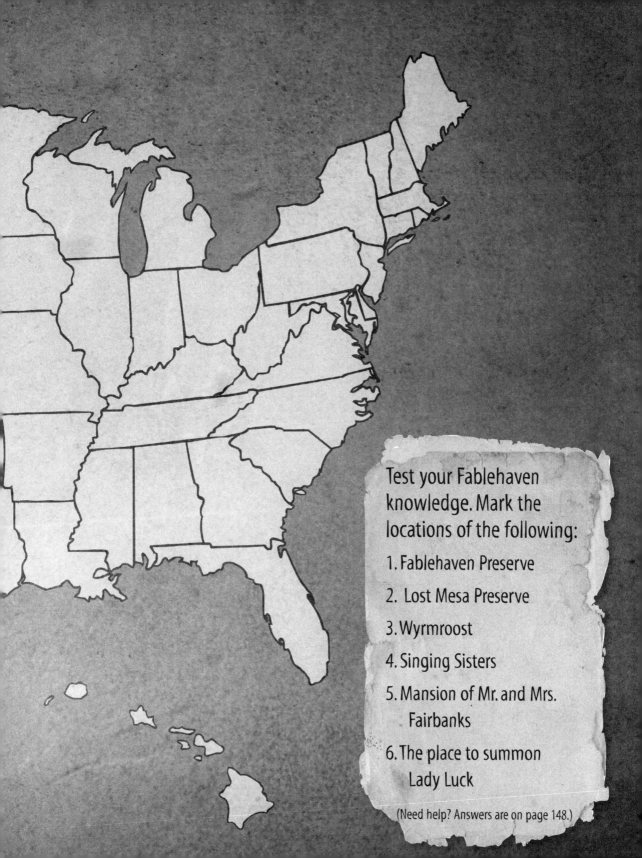

Test your Fablehaven knowledge. Mark the locations of the following:

1. Fablehaven Preserve
2. Lost Mesa Preserve
3. Wyrmroost
4. Singing Sisters
5. Mansion of Mr. and Mrs. Fairbanks
6. The place to summon Lady Luck

(Need help? Answers are on page 148.)

EXPRESS YOUR POTION EMOTION

1

2

5

6

On each numbered blank face, draw the expression listed below. Once you're finished, cover the potion list and and see if someone else can guess the right emotion based on your drawing.

Potions:
1. Sleepy
2. Scared

3. Courageous
4. Excited
5. Sad

6. Disappointed
7. Angry
8. Happy

3

4

7

8

SEND A BOTTLED MESSAGE

Caretaker Patton Burgess used a magic bottle to send a secret message to Seth. Write your secret message on the next page or on another piece of paper. What will you say? Who will you address it to? Now, find an empty bottle. Make sure the bottle can be sealed with a lid, cap or cork. Place your message inside. Leave the bottle where someone will find it. You may consider writing the words "Secret message inside" on the outside of the bottle.

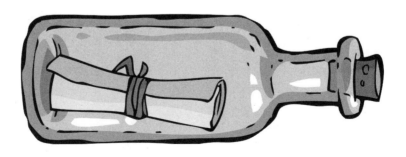

4:160:7:9

Seth acquired a figurine in the shape of an onyx tower from the Sky Giant Thronis. When placed upon the ground, and after you say the designated incantation, the model tower will enlarge into an elaborate stronghold. Draw what you think this castle fortress would look like.

Caretakers need to understand the creatures they oversee.

Pretend you're Hugo. Tell a family member you are their golem for 30 minutes and will do any tasks they require. Write down what you accomplish.

_____

_____

_____

Pretend you're a fairy. Find a mirror and admire your face, your eyes, and your hair. Say wonderful things about yourself. Write down the things you like about yourself.

_____

_____

_____

Pretend you're a centaur. Challenge somebody to a contest and show no fear! Record the details of the contest and whether or not you won.

_____

_____

_____

Pretend you're a sphinx. Create a riddle that people must answer correctly to get into your room. Record it here.

_____

_____

_____

Pretend you're a hermit troll like Bubda. Find a hiding place in your house or yard where you could live without being found. Describe it here.

_____

_____

Pretend you're a satyr. Write down excuses you could use to get out of work or school. Use them at your own risk!

_____

_____

_____

FAIRY FASHIONS

Draw and color fairy wings for each of the fairies below.

Make a Mini Megaphone

Zogo, the servant dwarf of Thronis the Sky Giant, rides a griffin and barks commands with his megaphone. Now it's your turn to create a megaphone like Zogo. Roll a piece of paper or cardstock into a tube. Tape and decorate your megaphone.

What three commands will you issue first?

1. _____

2. _____

3. _____

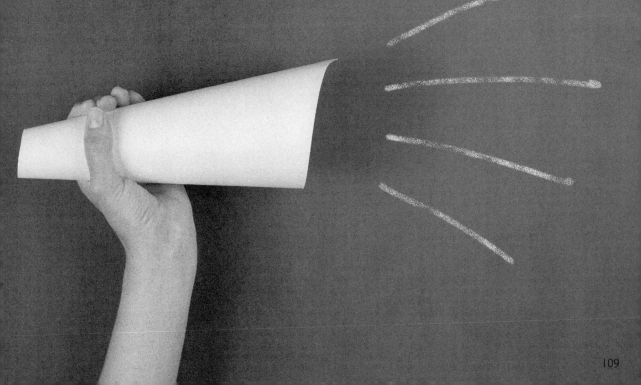

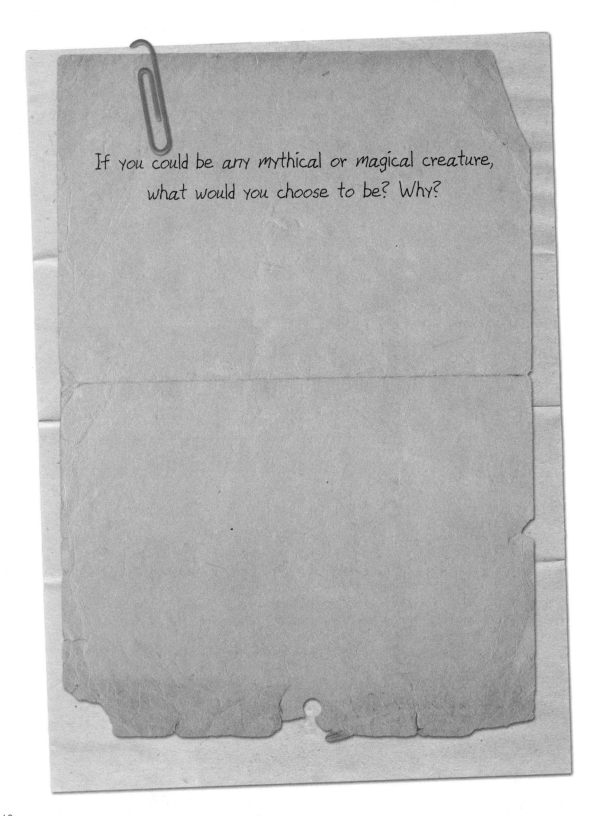

If you could be any mythical or magical creature, what would you choose to be? Why?

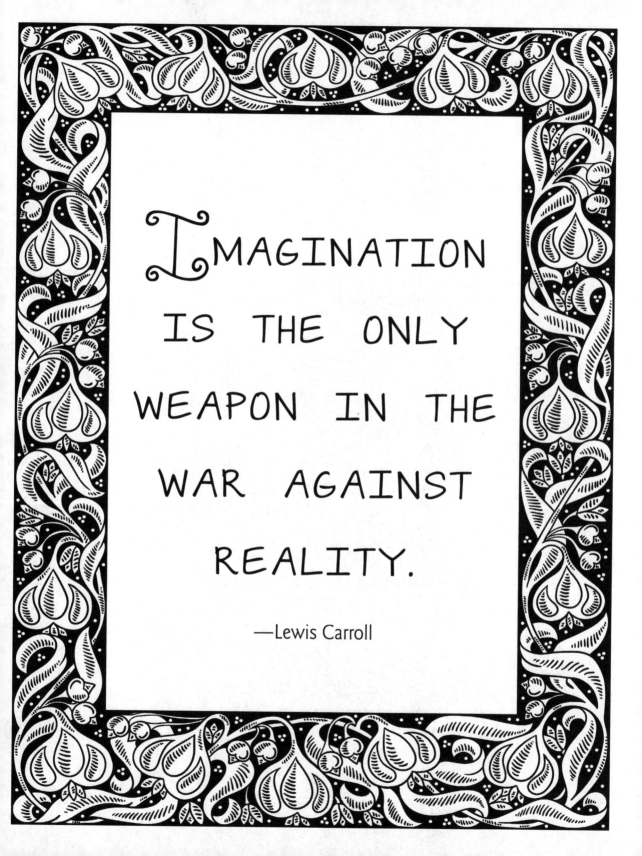

IMAGINATION IS THE ONLY WEAPON IN THE WAR AGAINST REALITY.

—Lewis Carroll

Write a Secret Message

Write a message that can be read when holding
this book upside down in front of a mirror.

1:338:1:5

LEARN TO MAKE WISE CHOICES

Lesson #3

GOOD CHOICES ARE NOT ALWAYS SAFE CHOICES. MANY WORTHY CHOICES INVOLVE RISK. SOME REQUIRE COURAGE.

—Patton Burgess
World's Greatest Adventurer

If you'd like, cut out the quote from
Patton Burgess on the previous page
and post it where you will see it often.

Be careful when coloring the mouth. All it takes is one bite . . .

These two pages are secret pages in your imagination journal. Write a message or a letter or place a thin, flat object between the pages and then seal the two pages together. Use glue to secure the corners and sides.

The more imagination
the reader has, . . . the more
he will do for himself. He will,
at a mere hint from the author,
flood wretched material with
suggestion and never guess that
he is himself chiefly making
what he enjoys.

—C. S. Lewis

FINISH THIS FABLEHAVEN ALPHABET

Words must be chosen from characters, creatures, places, or artifacts in the Fablehaven universe. (Hint: If you get stuck, *The Caretaker's Guide to Fablehaven* can help.)

A is for _____Astrid_____

B is for _____

C is for _____

D is for _____

E is for _____

F is for _____

G is for _____

H is for _____

I is for _____

J is for _____

K is for _____

L is for _____

M is for _____

N is for _____

O is for _____

P is for _____

Q is for _____

R is for _____

S is for _____

T is for _____

U is for _____

V is for _____

W is for _____

X is in _____

Y is for _____

Z is for _____

WHAT'S UP WITH HUGO?

Can you spot the differences between these two illustrations?

A

Circle the eleven things that are different between Hugo A and Hugo B.

B

Color the fantastical woods of Fablehaven. Trespassers beware.

Do not underestimate the young.

—Chu

Keys to the Demon Prison by Brandon Mull

Brandon

Stone Frog

DO NOT
FEED

*Brandon discovered a distant cousin to Olloch during a book tour
in Jakarta, Indonesia. Thankfully, he did not feed the frog.*

3:48:3:7

KNOW YOUR CREATURE TRACKS

In the spaces provided, draw the tracks that you think would correspond to the following creatures relative to a human footprint.

Nipsie

Imp

Griffin
(Hint: Its front tracks will be different from its back tracks.)

Hermit Troll

Human

Satyr

Zombie
(Hint: Most are missing toes.)

Naiad

Fog Giant

Golem (Hugo)

Centaur

Dragon

DRAW THE DUNGEON

Underneath the main house at Fablehaven is a dungeon. Slaggo and Voorsh, the goblins, cook the glop for the prisoners. Use your imagination and draw a map of the dungeon. Where is the goblins' cauldron located? How many hallways and cells will you include? List the prisoners in each cell. Are any cells empty?

where are the stairs that lead to the main house? Where is the Quiet Box located? Where is the door that leads to the Hall of Dread? And where is the narrowest hallway with no cell doors that leads to the circular room with a metal hatch in the center of the floor? Do you remember which prisoner is at the bottom of this cell? (Find the answer in *Rise of the Evening Star*, page 134.)

Never laugh at live dragons.

—J·R·R· Tolkien

5:71:27:6

Play Shadow Tag

During the shadow plague at Fablehaven, creatures were changed from light to dark. Organize a game of freeze tag where 1 to 2 players are light, 1 to 2 players are dark, and the others are neutral. If a neutral player is tagged by either light or dark, they become light or dark. A light player must be simultaneously touched by two dark players to turn dark. A dark player must be simultaneously touched by two light players to turn light. Play until all players are either light or dark. Invent additional rules as desired and record them in your journal at the back of this book.

Create a Time Capsule

Imagine if you had your own Chronometer and could travel fifty years into the future. Using the next page or another piece of paper, write a note to your future grandkids. What will you say to them? Will you try to warn them about something? How will you encourage them? Now find an airtight box or bottle and stick your letter inside along with a few trinkets from your life. Once your time capsule is sealed, you might consider burying it in your backyard or hiding it in your attic.

Make an Origami Olloch the Glutton

FOLLOW THE STEP-BY-STEP INSTRUCTIONS BELOW TO CREATE AN ORIGAMI OLLOCH THE GLUTTON.

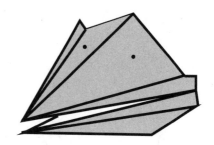

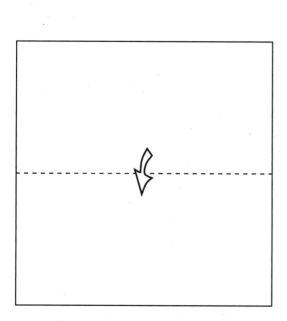

1. START WITH A SQUARE PIECE OF PAPER. FOLD PAPER IN HALF.

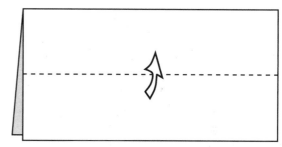

2. FOLD THE BOTTOM EDGE UP.

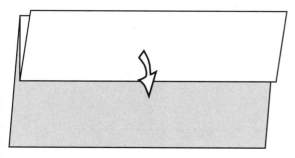

3. UNFOLD BOTTOM EDGE.

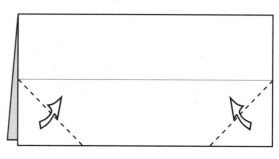

4. FOLD CORNERS ON DASHED LINES.

(CONTINUED ON NEXT PAGE)

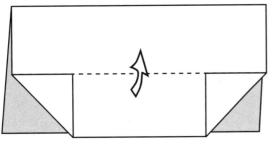

5. FOLD THE BOTTOM EDGE UP AGAIN.

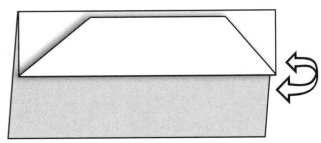

6. TURN PAPER OVER.

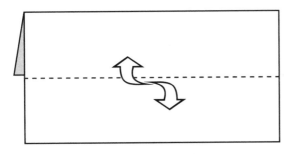

7. FOLD THE BOTTOM EDGE UP
AND THEN BACK DOWN.

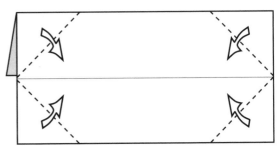

8. FOLD ALL CORNERS ON DASHED LINES.

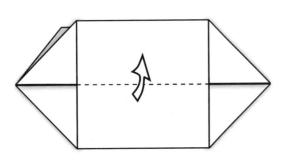

9. FOLD THE BOTTOM EDGE UP AGAIN.

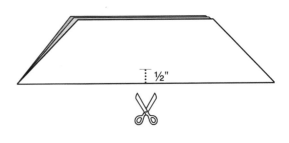

½"

10. MAKE A ½" CUT IN THE CENTER
OF THE MODEL.

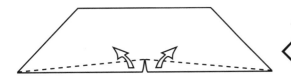

11. FOLD THE FLAPS ALONG THE DASHED LINE.

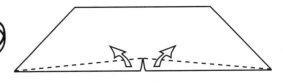

12. TURN THE MODEL OVER AND REPEAT.

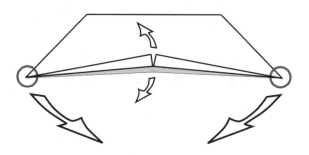

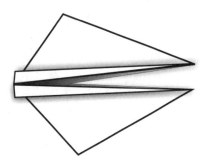

13. Pull the flaps apart at the middle and bring the end points together.

Finished model.

Olloch Game

Once you have made your Olloch, tear small pieces of paper and crumple them up into small balls. Have someone feed Olloch by tossing the balls to you. Try to snatch the pieces of paper in midair with your Olloch origami head. How many balls of paper can you gobble up without dropping any?

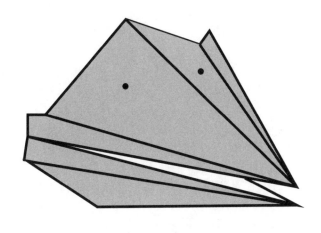

Unscramble these Fablehaven words

Note: All these creatures and magical items will appear in *Dragonwatch*.

Grando Stare _____

Locuus _____

Cakankps _____

Salivis _____

Hintsro _____

Blingbuts _____

Coinrun _____

Snipies _____

(Befuddled? Answers on page 148.)

4:493:25:11

SMART PEOPLE LEARN FROM THEIR MISTAKES, BUT THE REALLY SHARP ONES LEARN FROM THE MISTAKES OF OTHERS.

—Dale

Fablehaven by Brandon Mull

If you'd like, cut out the quote from Dale on the previous page and post it where you will see it often.

Picture This!

Find a picture of yourself and cut out your face. Place it over the face of the Astrid below. Then, find a picture frame and put your new Astrid picture inside the frame. Your friends will definitely be impressed!

My Imagination Journal

TRANSLATE THE SECRET MESSAGE

Let's _ _ _ _   _ _ _ _ _ _

_ _ _   _ _ _ _   _ _ _

_ _ _   _ _   _ _ _

_ _ _ _ _ _   _ _ _ _ _.

Answers. *Page 54:* First, take the leprechaun across Fablehaven. Return for the griffin. Leave the griffin and take the leprechaun with you. Leave the leprechaun and take the gold. Return for the leprechaun. *Page 79:* 1. The letter E. 2. A map. 3. A mushroom. 4. Nine. (Naiads can't drown, and they can't swim away in a pond.) *Page 82:* Singing Sisters. *Pages 98–99:* 1. Connecticut. 2. Arizona. 3. Just north of Montana border. 4. Missouri, island along the Mississippi River. 5. Atlanta, Georgia. 6. Hatteras Island, off the coast of North Carolina. *Page 140:* Dragon Tears, Oculus, Knapsack, Vasilis, Thronis, Stingbulb, Unicorn, Nipsies.

ACKNOWLEDGMENTS

A project like this Book of Imagination is much more collaborative than writing a novel. Though many talented people help get my novels ready to share with the world, with this project, a lot of people also helped directly with the content. Many different people contributed ideas and talent to help readers interact with the world of Fablehaven in new ways.

Chris Schoebinger deserves credit for coming up with the idea for this book and organizing the content. Without his leadership and effort, this book would not have happened. He's also the guy who accepted Fablehaven for publication in the first place. Thanks for everything, Chris!

Brandon Dorman illustrated the new dragon art for the cover as well as allowed us access to some of the Fablehaven art he has produced over the years, including images from *The Caretaker's Guide to Fablehaven*.

Steve Vistaunet created cool line art for the coloring pages. His interpretation of Olloch is awesome! And Chris Creek supplied the art for the "Draw a Dragon's Head" page.

James Fritzler created the Raxtus origami. That guy is a great paper engineer. After we discovered some of his origami online, he was happy to participate with this project.

I'd also like to thank the friends and family who shared ideas for this book, including Jason and Natalie Conforto, Adam Stevenson, Mary Mull, Sadie Mull, Summer Mull, Bryson Mull, Cherie Mull, Tiffany Mull, Pam Mull, and Gary Mull. Thanks to Cori Bailie, who tested *every* activity to make sure it worked.

Many thanks go to the Shadow Mountain design team, including Richard Erickson, Kayla Hackett, Rachael Ward, and especially Shauna Gibby, who customized each page. Shauna gets the Honorary Caretaker's Gold Star for her work on this project!

Others at Shadow Mountain also contributed to the success of this book, including Ilise Levine, John Rose, Lisa Mangum, Heidi Taylor, Julia McCracken, Sarah Cobabe, and Dave Brown. Their support and enthusiasm for this project has made a big difference.

I need to also thank my superagent, Simon Lipskar at Writers House, for his support and encouragement. And of course Mary and my kids for their continued support and understanding.

And I have to thank you, the reader, for trying out this experimental activity book. Hopefully it has been a fun experience. If you like it, let me know on Facebook or Instagram or Twitter. Just search "Brandon Mull."

Don't forget to keep an eye out for *Dragonwatch*, the first book in the sequel series to Fablehaven, starting in 2017. Also, if you haven't tried my Five Kingdoms series, I have been getting really positive responses from the kind of readers who enjoy Fablehaven.

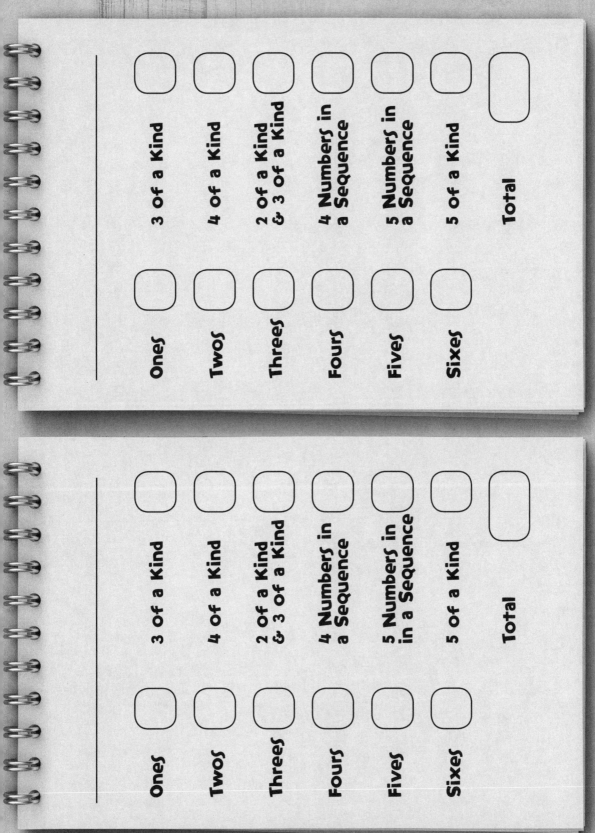

3 of a Kind

4 of a Kind

2 of a Kind & 3 of a Kind

4 Numbers in a Sequence

5 Numbers in a Sequence

5 of a Kind

Total

Ones

Twos

Threes

Fours

Fives

Sixes

3 of a Kind

4 of a Kind

2 of a Kind & 3 of a Kind

4 Numbers in a Sequence

5 Numbers in a Sequence

5 of a Kind

Total

Ones

Twos

Threes

Fours

Fives

Sixes

cut dark solid lines

mountain fold dotted lines

valley fold dashed lines

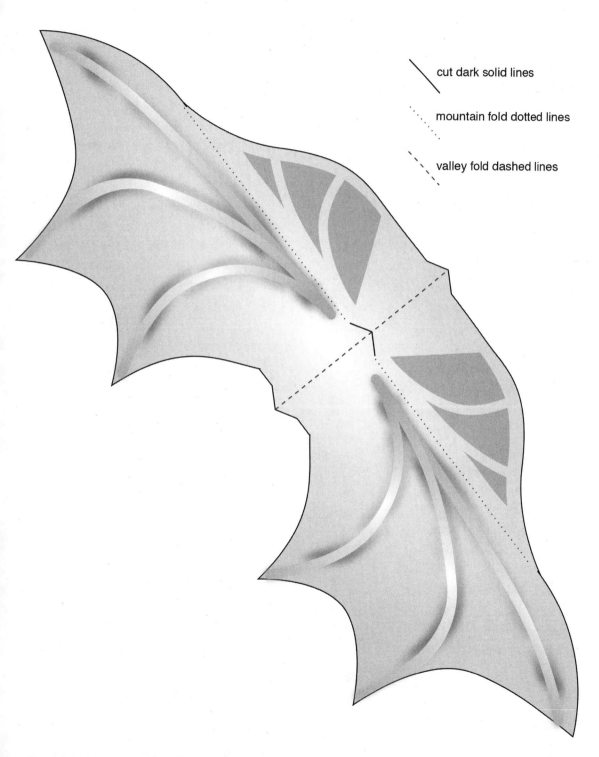

cut dark solid lines

mountain fold dotted lines

valley fold dashed lines

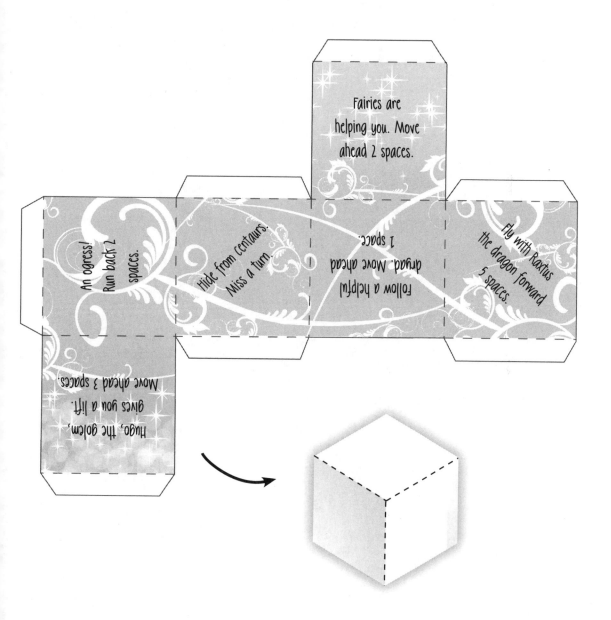

Fairies are
helping you. Move
ahead 2 spaces.

An ogress!
Run back 2
spaces.

Hide from centaurs.
Miss a turn.

Follow a helpful
dryad. Move ahead
1 space.

Fly with Raxtus
the dragon forward
5 spaces.

Hugo, the golem,
gives you a lift.
Move ahead 3 spaces.